Hey Diddle Diddle

Published in the United States of America by The Child's World®
1980 Lookout Drive • Mankato, MN 56003-1705
800-599-READ • www.childsworld.com

First published by Mathew Price Ltd.
5013 Golden Circle
Denton, TX 76208, USA.
Illustrations © 1990 Moira Kemp

Acknowledgments
The Child's World®: Mary Berendes, Publishing Director
Editorial Directions: E. Russell Primm, Editor; Lucia Raatma, Proofreader
The Design Lab: Kathleen Petelinsek, Art Direction and Design;
   Anna Petelinsek and Victoria Stanley, Page Production

Library of Congress Cataloging-in-Publication Data
Kemp, Moira.
  Hey diddle diddle / illustrated by Moira Kemp.
     p. cm. — (Favorite Mother Goose rhymes)
  Summary: Presents the classic nursery rhyme about a musical cat and his
fanciful friends.
  ISBN 978-1-60253-289-2 (library bound : alk. paper)
  1. Nursery rhymes. 2. Children's poetry. [1. Nursery rhymes.] I. Mother
Goose. II. Title. III. Series.
  PZ8.3.K34He 2009
  398.8—dc22   2009001555

ILLUSTRATED BY MOIRA KEMP

Hey diddle diddle,

the cat and the fiddle.

The cow jumped
over the moon.

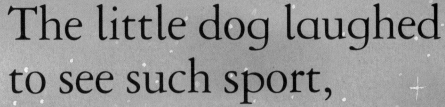

The little dog laughed
to see such sport,

and the dish ran
away with the spoon.

ABOUT MOTHER GOOSE

We all remember the Mother Goose nursery rhymes we learned as children. But who was Mother Goose, anyway? Did she even exist? The answer is . . . we don't know! Many different tales surround this famous name.

Some people think she might be based on Goose-footed Bertha, a kindly old woman in French legend who told stories to children. The inspiration for this legend might have been Queen Bertha of France, who died in 783 and whose son Charlemagne ruled much of Europe. Queen Bertha was called Big-footed Bertha or Queen Goosefoot because one foot was larger than the other.

The name "Mother Goose" first appeared in Charles Perrault's *Les Contes de ma Mère l'Oye* ("Tales of My Mother Goose"), published in France in 1697. This was a collection of fairy tales including "Cinderella" and "Sleeping Beauty"—but these were stories, not poems. The first published Mother Goose nursery rhymes appeared in England in 1781, as *Mother Goose's Melody; or Sonnets for the Cradle*. But some of the verses themselves are hundreds of years old, passed along by word of mouth.

Although we don't really know the origins of Mother Goose or her nursery rhymes, we *do* know that these timeless verses are beloved by children everywhere!

ABOUT THE ILLUSTRATOR

Moira Kemp has illustrated dozens of books for children, including many Mother Goose rhymes and activity songs. Kemp studied history at Oxford University in England, but she soon discovered a love for children's books and illustrations. She studied at the Camberwell School of Arts and Crafts. Her books have sold more than 5 million copies. She lives in Middlesex, England.